The Maestro Plays

ISBN 0-590-25470-7

Text Copyright © 1970 by Holt, Rinehart and Winston, Inc.
Illustrations Copyright © 1994 by Vladimir Radunsky.
All rights reserved. Published by Scholastic Inc.,
555 Broadway, New York, NY 10012,
by arrangement with Henry Holt and Company, Inc.

12 11 10 9 8 7 6 5 4   5 6 7 8 9/9 0/0

Printed in the U.S.A.

First Scholastic printing, September 1995

SCHOLASTIC INC.
New York   Toronto   London   Auckland   Sydney

The Maestro Plays

by Bill Martin Jr

pictures by
Vladimir Radunsky

THE MAESTRO PLAYS.
HE PLAYS PROUDLY.
HE PLAYS LOUDLY.

He plays slowly

He plays oh..ly.

He plays reachingly.

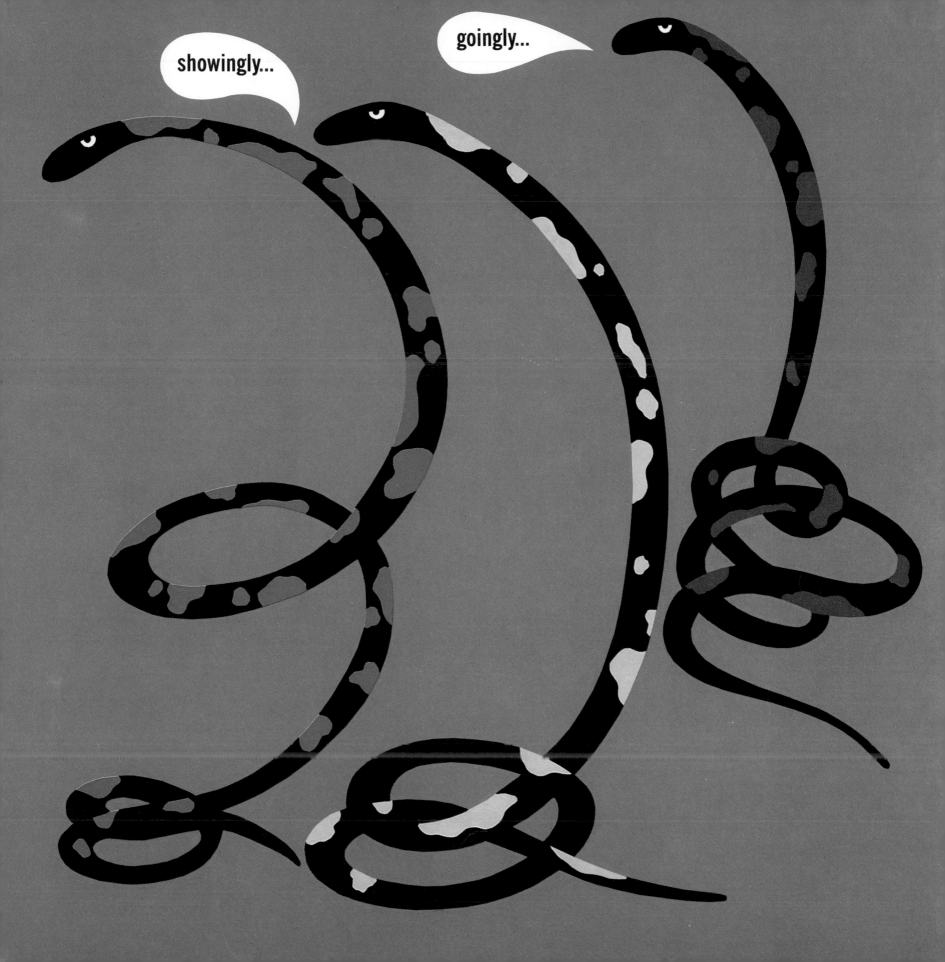

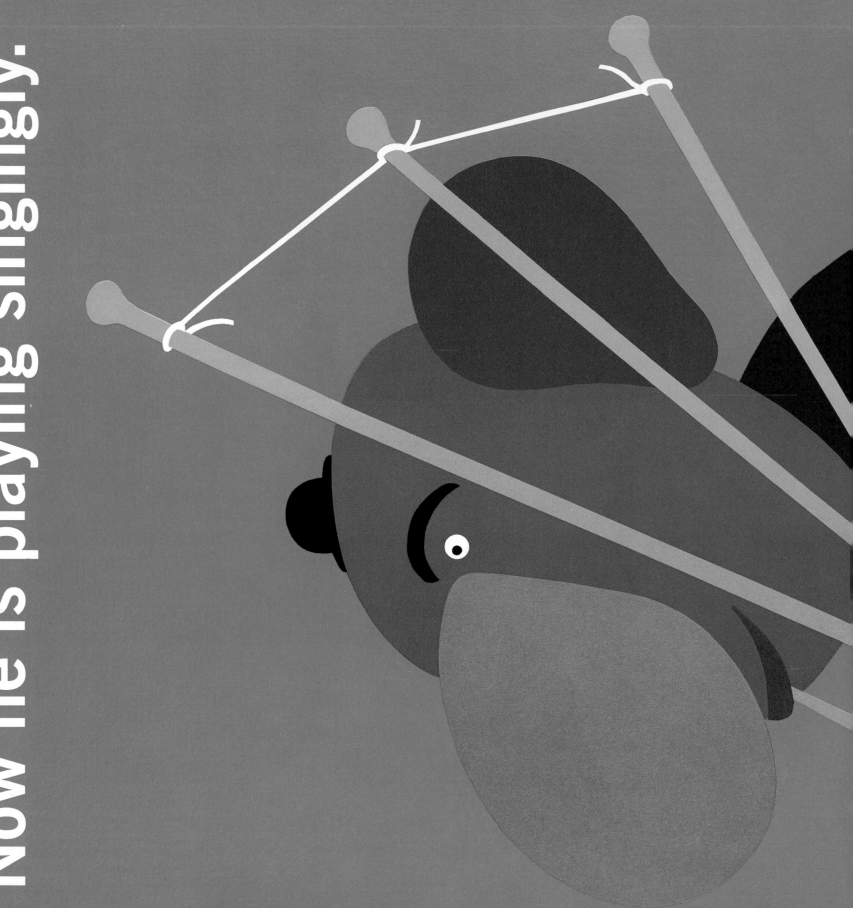

Now he is playing singingly.

He is playing ringingly,

wingingly . . .

swingingly

flingingly

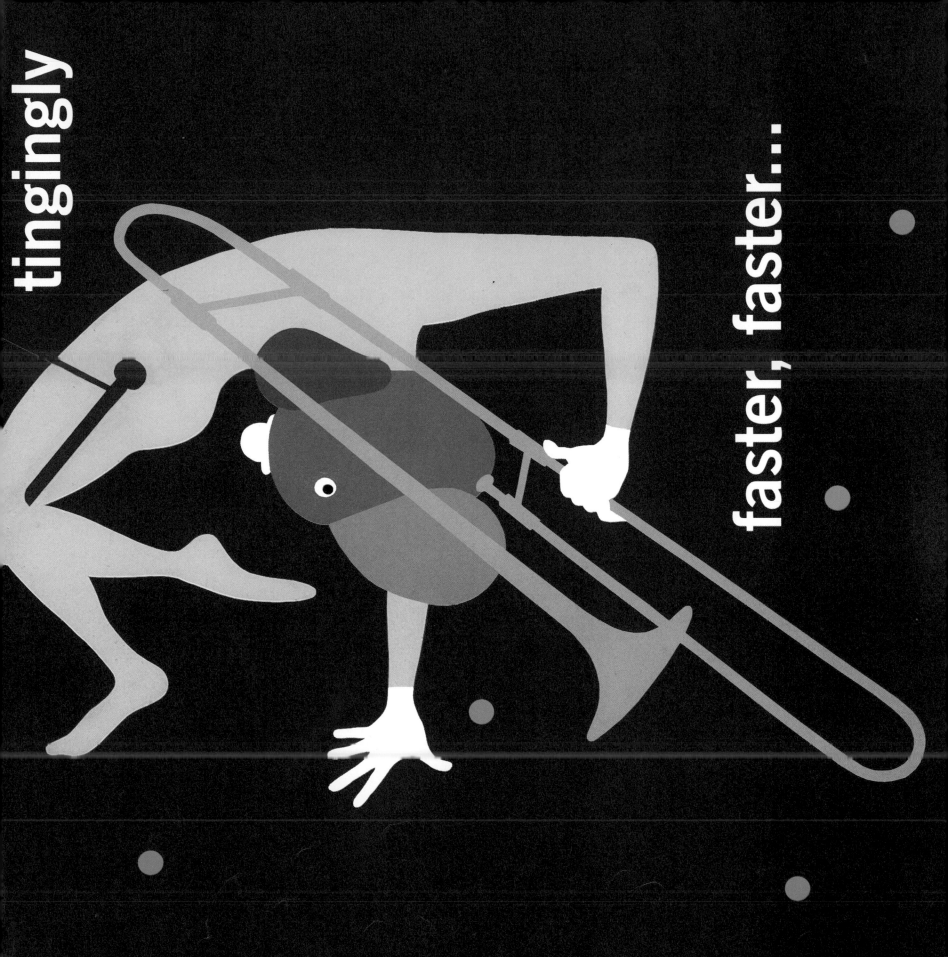

tingingly

faster, faster...

He plays busily.

He plays

dizzily.

He stops. He mops his brow.

The maestro begins

playing again mildly....

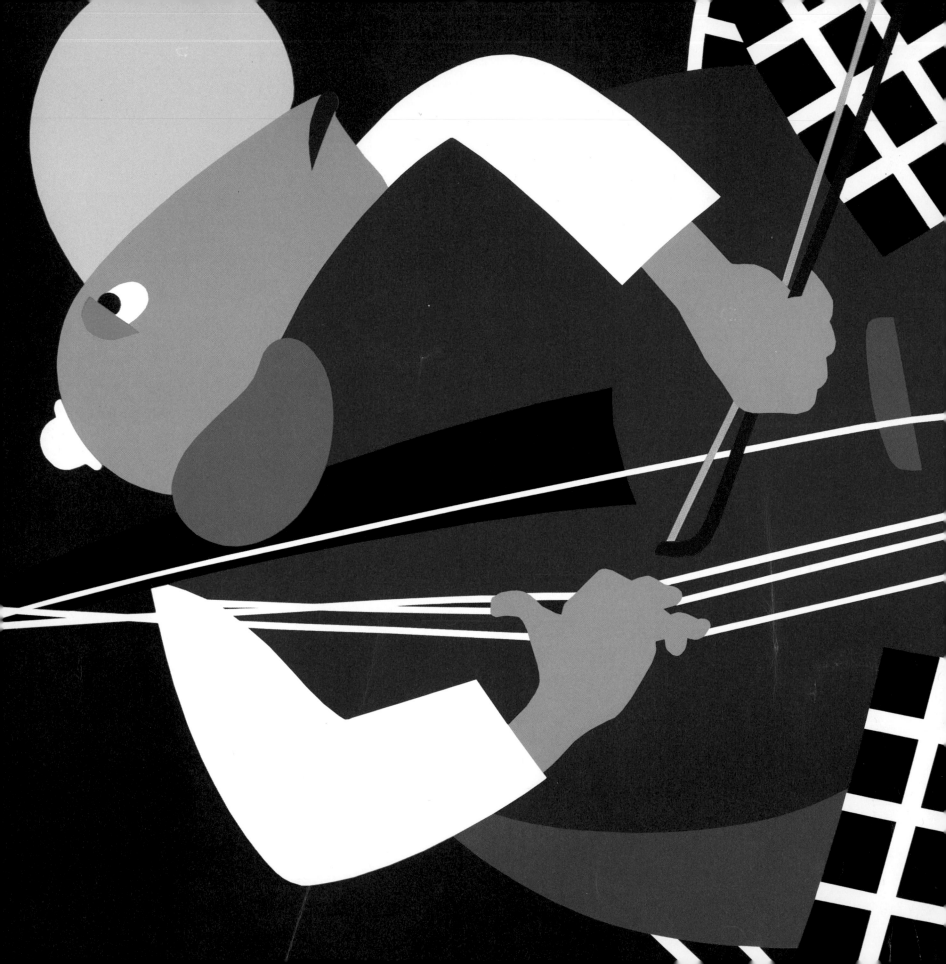

But suddenly he's playing wildly...

He bows furiously

He jabs!

He stabs!

He saws!

He slaps the strings.

He

plays

trrrr-r-r-r-ippingly.

He plays skippingly...

He plays sweepingly...
leapingly...
cheepingly...
faster...
faster.

He plays nippingly,

drippingly...

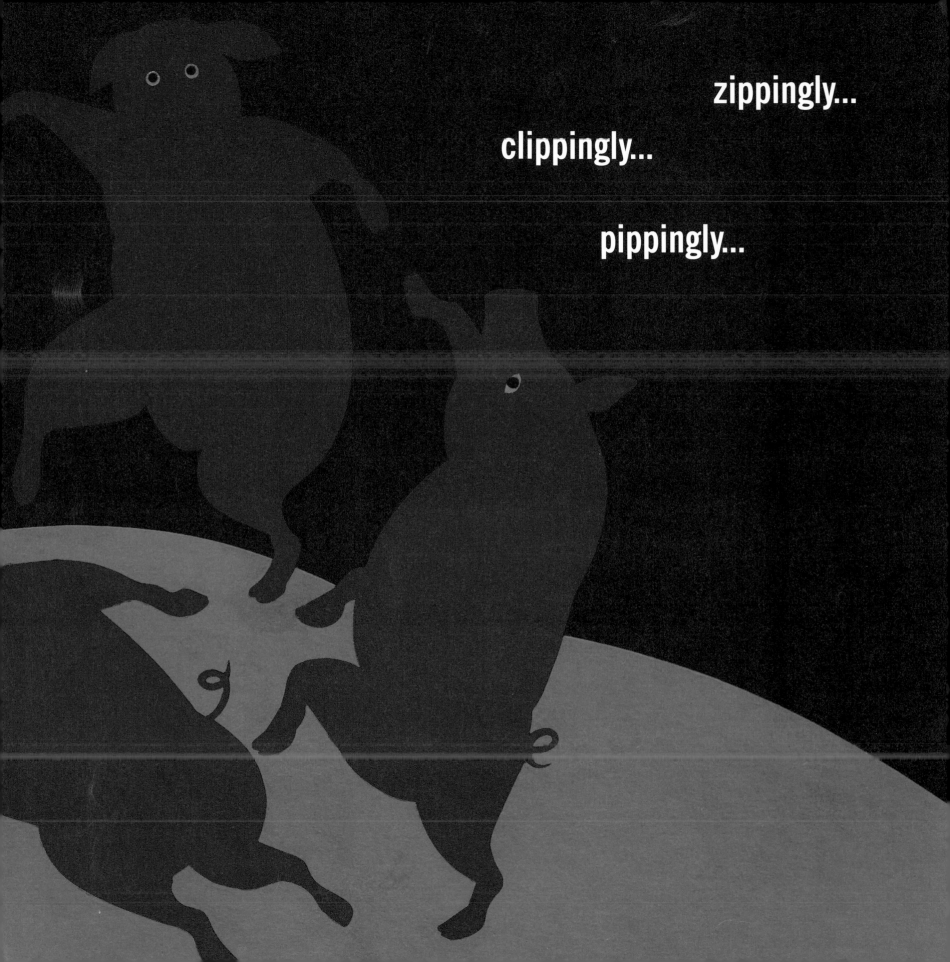

Rrrrriiiiiiiipppppiiinngly...